Caillou

Learns to Recycle

Text: Kim Thompson
Illustrations: Eric Sevigny, based on the television series

 chouette COOKIE JAR

It was snack time at day care.
Caillou and Leo were cleaning up
when they noticed a new bin in
the corner.
"What's that for? And what are
those pictures?" Leo wondered.
"I don't know. Let's ask
Ms. Martin," Caillou suggested.

"Ms. Martin, is that a new garbage can?" Leo asked.
"No, it's a recycling bin," she replied.
"What's recycling?" Caillou asked.
"I'm glad you asked, Caillou. That's the theme for today. Let's all sit down so we can talk about recycling."

"When we're finished with something and we throw it in the garbage can, where does it go?"

"To a big stinky pile of garbage," Leo exclaimed.

"That's right. And that garbage never gets used again."

"Recycling means using something more than once. When we put a bottle into the recycling bin, it goes to a factory where it's made into a brand-new bottle."

"So it gets used again," Caillou said.

"Yes," Ms. Martin said. "And again . . . and again."

"And again!" everyone joined in.

"Now I have something amazing to show you!" Ms. Martin said and left the room.

"What do you think it is?" Caillou whispered to Leo. Leo shrugged his shoulders.

"Ta-dah!" Ms. Martin rode in on her scooter, wearing a green tracksuit and waving rolls of toilet paper.

The children burst out laughing! Caillou asked, "What's so special about toilet paper?"

Ms. Martin pointed to some arrows on the wrapped toilet paper roll.

"The arrows tell me that this toilet paper was made from recycled paper, like old newspapers and cardboard boxes."

Caillou noticed something. "That's like the arrows you drew!"

"Yes, Caillou," Ms. Martin said. "This is the recycling symbol."

Next Ms. Martin showed them
a glass jar with the same arrows
on it.

"This jar is made of glass from
recycled juice and pop bottles.
See the arrows? So, just like the
paper, this glass can be used over
and over."

"And over!" the class called out,
laughing.

"Cans can be recycled, too!"
Ms. Martin continued. "The metal
is melted down and made into
new cans, paper clips, bicycles,
or even scooters!"
Caillou was impressed. "Your
scooter is made from cans? That is
amazing!"

"But the most amazing thing," Ms. Martin laughed, "is my tracksuit!"

Caillou wasn't so sure. It looked like an ordinary tracksuit to him. "When you put plastic bottles like Leo's juice bottle in the recycling bin, they can be made into new egg cartons, plant pots, yogurt containers, or even this tracksuit." Everyone agreed that really was amazing!

"Now do you know what these pictures on our recycling bin mean?" asked Ms. Martin. "That's to show us what to put in there. Glass, cans, paper and plastic," answered Caillou. "Right," said Ms. Martin. "Plastic! Like my juice bottle," exclaimed Leo. "My bottle's going to get used again and again!"

Ms. Martin had a T-shirt that was
made from plastic bottles, too.
"Who would like to help me put
our recycling into the new bin?"
she asked.

Caillou raised his hand. "Me,
please!"

"All right, Caillou. You can wear
this T-shirt and be my special
recycling helper for the day!"

Text: Kim Thompson
Illustrations: Eric Sevigny
Art Direction: Monique Dupras

The PBS KIDS logo is a registered mark of PBS and is used with permission.

We acknowledge the financial support of the Government of Canada through
the Canada Book Fund for our publishing activities.

Canadian Patrimoine
Heritage canadien

We acknowledge the support of the Ministry of Culture and Communications
of Quebec and SODEC for the publication and promotion of this book.

SODEC
Québec

Bibliothèque et Archives nationales du Québec and Library
and Archives Canada cataloguing in publication

Thompson, Kim, 1964-
Caillou recycles
(Ecology club)
For children aged 3 and up.

ISBN 978-2-89718-027-0

1. Recycling (Waste, etc.) - Juvenile literature. I. Sévigny, Éric. II. Title.
III. Series: Ecology club.

TD794.5.T463 2013   j363.72'82   C2012-941687-8

RECYCLED
Paper made from
recycled material
FSC® C103304

The use of entirely recycled paper
produced locally, containing
chlorine-free 100% post-consumer
content, saved 16 mature trees.

Printed in Canada
10 9 8 7 6 5 4 3 2 1   CHO1866   JAN2013

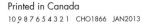